For Marin,
who first asked the question.

- HN -

For Adam.

- NR -

For information, contact Downtown Books Publishing,
66 Genesee Street, Auburn, NY 13021.

Author photo for Heidi Nightengale by Marcus DeVoe.
Author photo for Nancy Romano by Tom Hannig.

ISBN: 978-0-692-27019-6

First Edition: 2014

downtownbooksandcoffee.com

What Fragrance is the Moon?

2017
For Jacob~
who is the
fragrance of
The Future!
♥ -HN

Written by
Heidi Nightengale

Illustrated by
Nancy Romano

Auburn, NY

“Mama, what fragrance is the moon?”

“The moon is the fragrance of peppermint sticks
and the golden meringue of a lemon pie.”

“Mama, what fragrance is the wind?”

"The fragrance of the wind is fresh laundry hung from a line or warm from the dryer."

"Mama, what fragrance is magic?"

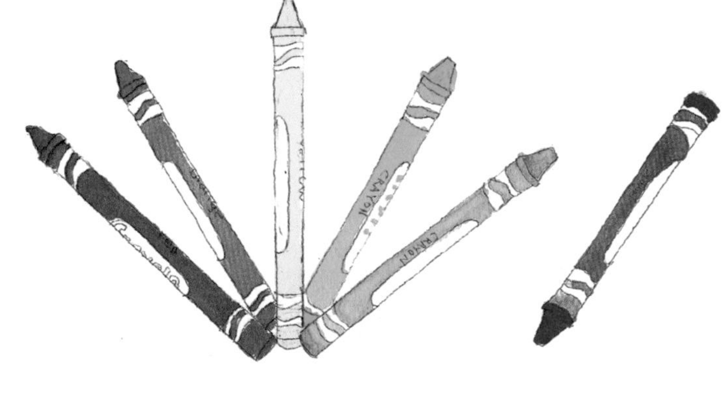

"The fragrance of magic is the
red, orange, yellow, green, blue and purple
of your crayons and *your* pictures."

COOKIES

"Mama, what fragrance is the song of birds?"

"The song of birds is the fragrance of blueberries, apple pies and a handful of raisins."

"Mama, what fragrance is snow?"

"The fragrance of snow is like a crisp, crunchy apple."

PLAYD
PLAY DO

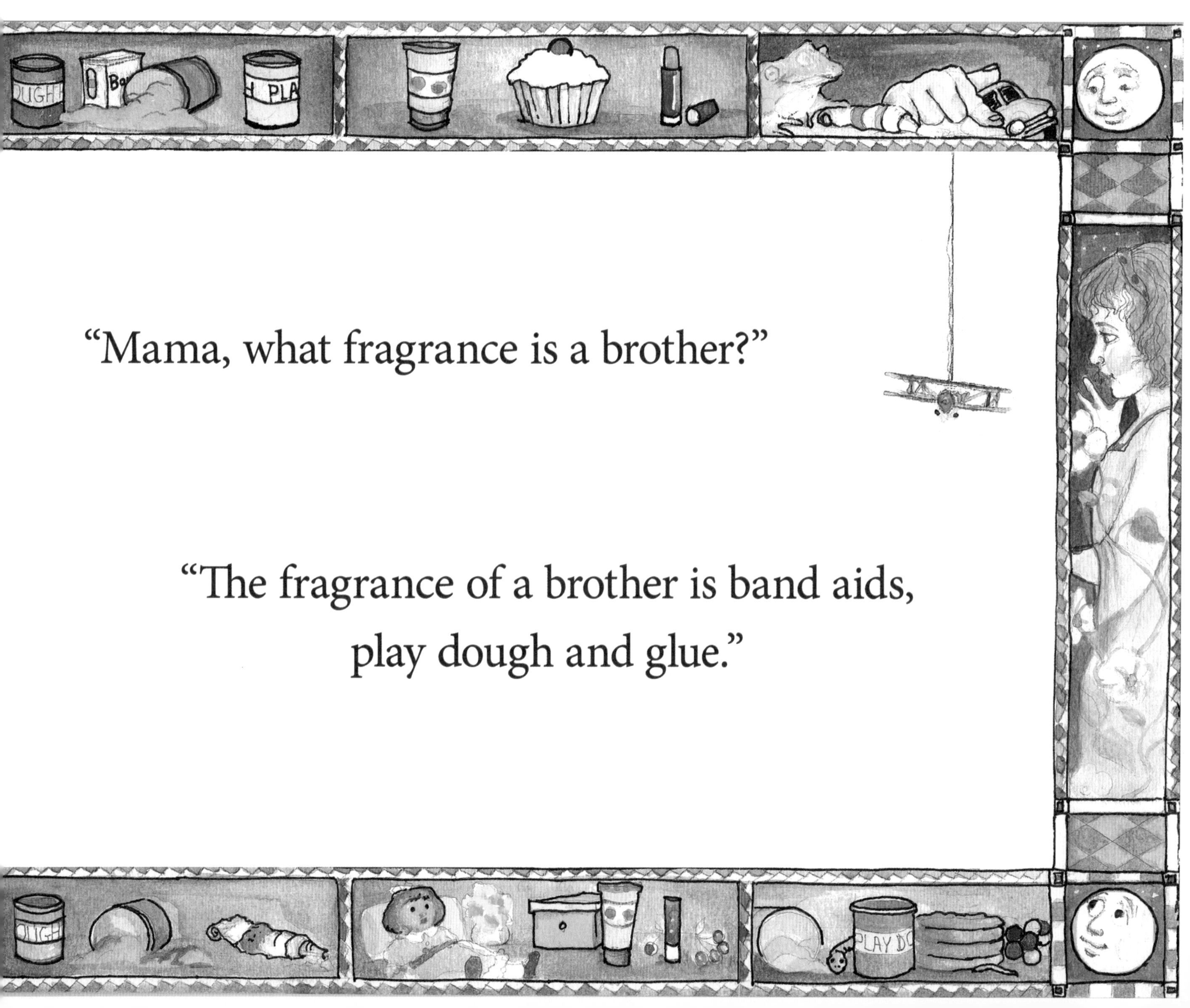

"Mama, what fragrance is a brother?"

"The fragrance of a brother is band aids, play dough and glue."

"Mama, what fragrance is a sister?"

"The fragrance of a sister is cherry lip gloss, melon hand cream and vanilla cupcakes."

OUGH
H PLA
OUGH
PLAY DO

"Mama, what fragrance is a watermelon seed?"

CAMP

"The fragrance of a watermelon seed is
like a campfire's embers."

"Mama, what fragrance is the sun?"

"The fragrance of the sun is the bite of the first warm strawberry plucked from the patch."

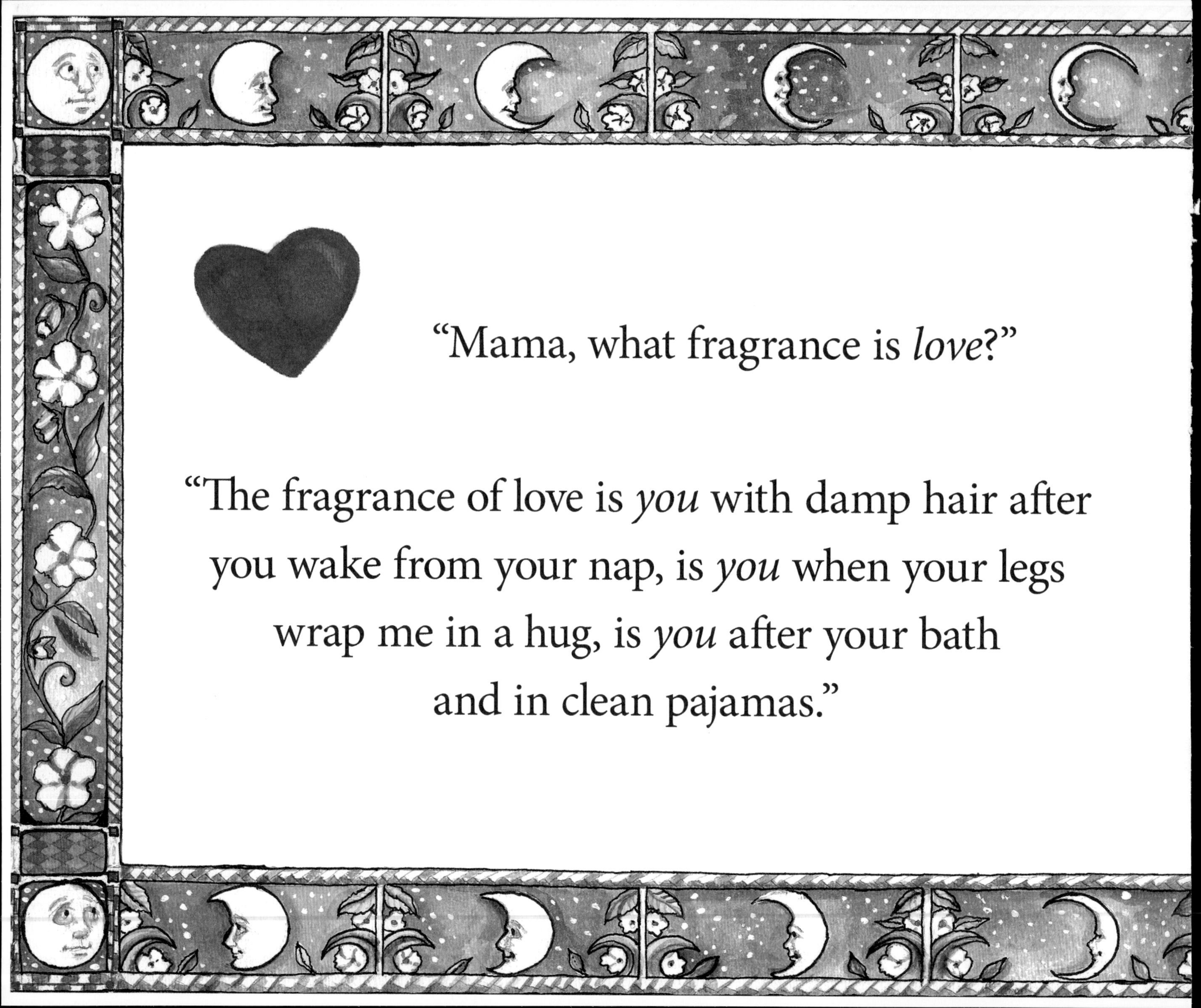

"Mama, what fragrance is *love*?"

"The fragrance of love is *you* with damp hair after you wake from your nap, is *you* when your legs wrap me in a hug, is *you* after your bath and in clean pajamas."